IT'S BETTER IF YOU DON'T KNOW

A Collection of Short Stories

Raissa Batra

INDIA • SINGAPORE • MALAYSIA

Copyright © Raissa Batra 2023
All Rights Reserved.

ISBN 979-8-89186-515-0

This book has been published with all efforts taken to make the material error-free after the consent of the author. However the author and the publisher do not assume and hereby disclaim any liability to any party for any loss damage or disruption caused by errors or omissions whether such errors or omissions result from negligence accident or any other cause.

While every effort has been made to avoid any mistake or omission this publication is being sold on the condition and understanding that neither the author nor the publishers or printers would be liable in any manner to any person by reason of any mistake or omission in this publication or for any action taken or omitted to be taken or advice rendered or accepted on the basis of this work. For any defect in printing or binding the publishers will be liable only to replace the defective copy by another copy of this work then available.

To Rabbani, my twin sister, for when we no longer have bedrooms across the kitchen

And for everything and more

Table of Contents

How to Listen to a Story

I made a promise that I would never sugarcoat things, especially not this. Maybe it's too straightforward; maybe you'll need to clutch your chest because when I told you to lean in, you thought you would be told a secret. But all I told you was the end. Maybe you'll step away from me for a second, or for an hour, or maybe you were never even close to me, to begin with. What matters is, I cannot control how people will react. However, I can control how I tell my story. Or whatever is left of it, anyway.

The thing is, anything can be a story but only if you make it so. If I were to say, my mother died when I was twenty, she would still be dead. But, if I were to tell you that she only ever wore shades of red, you would laugh and she would be there in each word, each twinkle in the eye, each question that followed. I do not want you to ask me how she died. I want you to ask how she is still alive—how every time I bleed, it feels like she is still here and how I'll never have strawberries covered in chocolate even though they used to be my favourite because it would mean hiding the red. A story can be tragic, but I would tell you and I would not want you to cry because I would cry, too. But I would tell you because I want to watch it come alive once again. Anything can be a story but only if you make it so. And what I want is for people to listen closely.

I am lying on my deathbed. There is nothing that I can do about it. I don't think I would have done anything even if I could. There are some days when I cannot even sleep because I feel like I will miss all the hours I could have lived. That does not make me desperate for a second chance but a person who wants to play out her past and then leave in peace. I want to scream out that I have lived, and it should be enough. I want to scream that I have a story even when I was the only person in the room. And stories can be tragic but they still deserve to be listened to.

I have too many friends who have probably forgotten about me. I don't know if I should even call them my friends. But I guess when you're on your deathbed, the world seems softer, the people kinder. And yes, I have been too harsh on myself and there's a point in your life when you regret it. But, if I could change something in my life, it would be the things I've regretted that I shouldn't have, and the things I should have probably regretted. But at one point, you just run out of things you can say, and not because you actually do. It's just that you stop trying. And this is the last time people will probably talk about me. And I have come to terms with that. Because if there is one thing I will never regret, is the last days of my life. I don't even know if you feel regret after you are dead, but all I know is that I cannot bear to carry this hurt inside me anymore. I learnt this far too late.

I haunted my old school when I wasn't even dead, and I'll probably add two more schools to haunt when I'm dead. Because I have moved places maybe twice or thrice, I forget. Sometimes things just blend together, but I guess it happens more when you know you're about to die. At least that is what is happening to me. I am in such a hurry to remember every moment of my life that I get too anxious about whether I'll ever be able to get through it all before it's too late. I used to be getting through high school, but then I was barely getting anywhere. Sometimes you are just caught up in the race of it all that you forget you're caged.

It is quite hard to get out of this system that defines success as a meter. How far above the social or work ladder are you? That is what I thought success was until my mother died. Getting out of bed seemed hard, and when I did, I felt successful. I finally learnt how to cook my family's recipes. I was too scared to cry over my mother's handwriting. I did cry, but I didn't spoil the neat pages. My dishes were too salty, but at least I used the recipes. I felt successful. What the world had told me about success was a cage. I didn't have the keys but at least I could slide out through the gaps.

I have moved places maybe twice or thrice; this is the longest I have stayed somewhere. And yet, it feels like I'm still stuck in my hometown. The harshness in my tongue could only belong there; my friends used to hate me, and to them, I'm already dead. The thing is, I have moved on. Just because I hold grudges like I used to hold myself when I would cry in the middle of the night, does not mean that I am still hung up over it. But, what I saw and heard made me naive at one point and I hate them for giving me hope. But then, later, I realised that no one would come through. I would always be screaming into the void. If I were to ever talk about how all the incidents made me feel, they would walk away. And now, it's the end for me. I do not know how to feel. A few weeks ago, I cried uncontrollably. But the lights seem too bright now, the crowds too loud. With each breath, it feels like I'm forgetting how to breathe. This does not feel like giving up, it feels like acceptance. As if my body knows that sometimes, it's better to stay than to run, better to close my eyes for longer than to look at the beeping monitor beside my hospital bed.

Death is a funny thing. No matter how rich or poor or famous you are, this inevitably is what makes us equal—a place where the line is drawn, and no one can cross it. There is no clever way around it. Death is a funny thing, but no one is laughing. Instead, they are doing whatever it takes to distance themselves from it. And yet there are slight smiles below dark circles, as if, if it is caught, they will never be seen again. Death humour is all around us, just not in front of me, because I am dying.

My hand falters on the wrapping of the salty pasta I am having for lunch. I met a nurse earlier; she told me that she had seen death many times. It stuck with me because it made me feel less alone. I had known she would never tell a dying person about death but I had insisted. Death is like stepping into the unknown; I wanted to do whatever I could to make myself feel less nervous. The crying stopped weeks after I found out I would die; I have said that before but the nervousness never went away. I have forgotten how to read; my mind seems like a stranger, and I cannot escape the boredom each day brings me. I take the fork to eat the pasta. I hope the nurse comes back.

I have hated how things always fell through; how wherever I went, people had to say something. I thought eventually my anger would fix it. It never did. I would like to plan out my part in this but I found out that it was never about me. When people feed you words on knives, you learn to share them with those around you. When people tell others why they should hate you, they try to see for themselves. And then they expect me to cry as if I never had a choice in this matter. See, anger is useful, but it wasn't in this case; so silence seemed better. You took what you took but you didn't pay attention to the fact that I stole your remarks and locked them within me. I took your knives and put them in the kitchen drawer; I took your whispers and I painted my bedroom. It wasn't to make me weaker but to show myself that I was so much stronger than you.

My entire life, I have felt like I needed space. I just wanted to get away from it all. My entire life I have been running, but it never feels like I am getting anywhere. The past did not stay in the past, and I did not stay in one place for too long. Are people inherently good or bad? I never stayed long enough to notice. Until now. Bare walls, bare room, I cannot bear to be with myself. At this moment, at a time when I cannot stop thinking about the inevitability of each action, each breath, each step that brings me closer to my mother. A life of contemplation was always the best one for me. But now, I just want someone to hate me so that I do not notice that I hate myself. This is not because I am insecure;

it is because when you're on your deathbed, while the world seems softer, your breath seems harsher. As if you're trying to hang on to something that you have felt was never yours. But, I did say I would not regret my last days.

When people said treasure your life, I guess they never meant the people in it as well; they meant just the fact that you're breathing and well. I have always loved the rain not because it seemed like the world cried but because it seemed like a new start. I had a friend once, who whispered in my ear all the conversations she had heard on the bus to school and she whispered about me to someone else. I got to know about the old couple on the bus and the stoic man in a suit going to work. I got to know how old the couple was and how the man looked poor but I never knew that the old couple used to share their food and that the man had found out his grandmother was dead on the way to work until I took the same bus to school. She whispered about me. I left her in the chemistry classroom; it had been raining.

I made a promise that I would never sugarcoat things because I had hurt the same way. If you say no by saying I don't know, they'll think it's a yes. When the touches were over, I told myself that it was okay but it should not have been. It should have risen from me instead of lodging in my throat; I was right. He was wrong. It was over but it was like a story I could never finish until I splashed my face with cold water and realised it was never my fault. I drove by his house, but I was still so far from him, still above him. If he took the 'I don't know' as a yes, it wasn't my fault; it was his. And if I say no in my sleep now, it does not mean that I am crazy; it only means that I am human.

I could write a book about my past, but I never did because it would rip me open. Keeping it in my mind felt better, but with each breath, I feel like I'm losing bits and pieces of who I used to be. All I can hope is that the pain will go away. People can say and do a lot of things, but take the good things in you, never the bad. I used to have many hobbies; these days, it's watching the birds outside my window. I could write a book because I have written one. It was in the drawer with all the pills and coupons before I was moved to the hospital room. The apartment building burned down soon after.

The friends that never lasted, the mothers that were dead, the breaths that came shorter now and the hospital walls that will be left. I was all alone, in a body that was old and frail but had been soft to the touch; the breaths in my hospital room stuck to me. The regrets had piled up too much; my body had been a vessel, and my last days had been busy with just draining it out.

I look outside my window; the softness of the sound of rain on the windows fills the room. My unfinished pasta lies on the table beside me, my thoughts so far from the hospital room. My past is right there where I left it but it seems next to me now. As if I have seen all that I could see, thought about all there was in life, seen my mom so many times in each memory, and loved the world so much that I was finished loving it. As if I had too many rainy days that I wanted the sun now. As if I had lived through noise too much that I deserved the silence. As if with every step I took, it would bring me closer to my mother and with every step the nurse took she would hear the flat line.

Listen to the Chants in the Hospital Room (Power)

It started with power, as it always does in this world. It rose deep within the newborn baby, chanting and slowly rising.

Power.

Power.

Power.

The baby didn't know any words. But power: it wasn't just a word. It was a feeling slowly washing over you. It would seep through the bones and the veins and harden slowly. It washed over you slowly but steadily. It was an idea; a being. The cry rose from the baby—a shout, a scream and a sudden burst of tears. There was power in crying too, in raising your voice, in showing weakness while knowing it made you stronger. But the baby didn't know that. Not now, maybe never. But it only knew power. Power, in its most vicious form.

The parents hadn't asked for the gender before. The doctor said over the crying baby, 'It's a girl,' and left noticing the tension in the room.

The woman asked the husband, 'Do you feel sad?' There was power in that dynamic. The woman almost sounded scared of her husband. But there was power in being scared, too, and still speaking through the fear.

With a sharp whisper, the husband—now a father—said, 'She will have to do.'

Power. What man is taught to use against baby girls crying in the hospital room and women who walk alone at night. They use it to silence the chant of power inside women until it is nothing but a whisper. Power bites sharp in the small absence of it. From small bodies to tall women.

She will have to do. She will have to do. She will have to do.

Perhaps this was the chant inside of the baby. *She will have to do*—learn to do—without power until she is brave enough to answer what the power whispered in the back of her mind. She will have to do until then. She will have to understand what it means when people have power and to be the one living without it. There is power in that, because power is vicious, but only if you continue to let it be.

A new cry rose from the newborn baby and filled the room. Hardening.

Power may do well in her hands.

Listen to the Door Slamming (The Other Side of the Door)

I left her at my doorstep that night; it was pouring. She told me she needed me. Again.

I knew I had to shut the past behind me. I could feel it slipping. But I was scared of that commitment because I knew I would run back to all the people I used to know just because it was comfortable. I had a dream the other day. I died without ever accomplishing what I wanted. I wanted to be a writer; I was a writer, and I still am. But why did it feel like everything I had done to get there was disappearing? As if everyone who knew me was turning their back on me. And I would have to run back to her.

I didn't realise being dependent on someone took away so much of your energy, until someone leaned on my shoulder. There were some days when I wished I was invisible. But there was something else that I wished for even more. I needed people to know about me and I couldn't do it if I lived in her shadow. Who she was, I needed to forget.

—

Three years later, at twenty-one, my book got published. I was halfway there. And then the next year, I climbed further. I was not just a writer, people even knew about me. They needed me. I was on the top. But now, at thirty, I keep running back to my past, proposing a nice dinner with all my ghosts I had vowed to keep buried. I don't realise what this feeling is. Everything needs to come crashing down to rebuild me again.

I guess to figure out why I keep running back to my past, I needed to know what was there that I left buried.

I used to go to this cafe when I was fifteen. I used to buy a cup of coffee and just sit there and write. Or fantasise about writing. With everything that was going on in my life, I needed my writing to be perfect. I didn't know how to be good. I didn't know how to learn. I was seventeen when my father died. I cried but it was not the wetness of my cheeks; rather, it was the wetness of the ink bleeding the sadness out of me. It was a rough time for me. My father was dead, and I had not improved my writing skills because I never wrote.

At sixteen, I was at the cafe when I met her. She was there, with her cup of coffee, and I knew she was a writer. She saw me looking, and I tried to run away. It had been embarrassing, I never figured out why. When I try to sleep at night now, all I can see is her face that day—when she said she could help me.

I wonder if I had realised that the glint in her eyes was anything but compassion. I wonder if I had run away quicker. I wonder if I had looked away at the first glance. What if I had never showed up at the cafe. I wonder.

When I turned seventeen, I finally wrote something. It was hard; she was there. Maybe it helped, maybe it was just me. But it left me exhausted. I felt lost; everyone seemed to be leaving me, and even in summer, all I felt was cold. But she was there. Though I hate her now, she was there when no one else was. And for me, that was all that mattered then. And also the fact that she told me she would help me with my writing.

Eighteen and nineteen, I would later remember as a time where the only thing I did was write. Most of it was bad. She said she had seen something in me that day when she saw me first; she was struggling to find that something right now. It pushed me; I guess it would later prove to be counterproductive. But, at that moment, I was writing. And I could finally see some improvement. How much growth happened in those moments is not puzzling to me now; I know it was minimal. I wonder who helped me. Had it even been her or was it just me all along? I guess I'll never know. I don't know myself now, and I didn't know myself then.

Twenty had been a pivotal point in my life. I found out she had been exploiting me. My writing, my voice; it seemed hers. Don't be her friend, my brain had said repeatedly the day I found out. My heart wanted to give her a second chance. I would realize later that I had been giving her second chances since the day she met me at the cafe. Yes, she had been my literary agent, but she had been someone familiar. I was too scared to leave something I had known for so long. I had found comfort in familiarity and in the back of my head, I knew it would come to hurt me.

I won an award at twenty-one. I went up to the stage but I forgot to say her name. I used to think I would never be able to escape her. That was the first time I had a taste of freedom. And I vowed to be free. Because all I could feel were invisible shackles and her name on my lips every time I would be interviewed. It was painful. Each morning in the shower, I would wonder if it were possible a person could bleed dry because of crying so much.

At twenty-two, I left her in our shared hotel room halfway through my book tour. I did not realise it would become that much of a scandal. People did not recognize me because of my books; they recognized me because I was me and because I had left her at the desk, halfway through booking our flight to another city somewhere.

It was the saddest part of the right thing to do. But, leaving was like taking a breath of fresh air. The world had seemed so welcoming. I had to start all over again, but I did not feel scared. I felt hopeful.

At twenty-three, I published another book. I didn't expect it to do better, but I wanted it to. It was supposed to be a silent protest. I could and would be a better writer without her. Now, I don't understand why I continued to seek her validation even when she was no longer there. Seventeen-year-old me would have understood. But at this age, I don't think I ever will.

I tried writing again, at thirty. I could not bring myself to touch my pen, or even my computer. I simply sat with a cup of tea. Exactly like I used to, at the cafe. But this time, I was all alone with the memories of my past—all the people who hated me. I have never been one for tradition; it was all so unnecessary. I knew I could not afford to be dependent on someone again. I would not write just because someone told me I should. I would write because of me and who I was. I had to push myself harder, I understood this much. But I could not shake this feeling that sometimes it felt like I had become the best I could ever be. That I would push myself harder but I would remain stuck forever.

I have made many mistakes, I know. I am not perfect, nor will I ever be. But with my writing, I cannot help but feel that with every mistake I make, I become an even worse writer, an even worse version of myself. It has haunted me ever since that cafe. It haunts me still.

My last week of being thirty-one, I had a sudden urge to read the newspaper. I was hungry for a story. But what I saw was not what I had expected. She had lived in the neighbouring town all this time; she had been so close and I hadn't even had a clue. And she had died in a car crash; it had been entirely her fault. She left nothing but a huge pile of debt and a woman who still had trouble running away from her past. I burned the newspaper but I still could not stop thinking about all the "what-ifs" at night. It was progress, but whether it is eighteen feet or eight feet under water, both are considered drowning. I still needed a win.

When I'm alone, which is most of the time, I like to befriend all the possibilities that could have ever been. Some people call it unhealthy. In some of my weak moments, I might even say that myself. However, I cannot bring myself to stop. Because a part of me still wishes she was nice. A part of me still wishes to be a naive girl who was never tricked. Because not every moment with her had been painful, and that made me hate her less. This makes me want to scream. Would it not be easier if my emotions were just extreme? Couldn't I either love her or hate her? But in a world where things always seemed black or white, everything was just grey to me. And so, I'm a mess, still wishing, still hoping. Still tasting the coffee from the cafe fifteen years ago, because it tastes a bit bitter, a bit sweet. I should go drink some water, I think.

See, my mother was never around. I needed my father but he died. I couldn't even bring myself to say goodbye. So she was all I had. And now when I try to remember the woman from the cafe, all I try to focus on is the glint in her eye. As if she knew something that I didn't. As if she would always know something that I would never figure out. Be that as it may, she may have made me a better writer, she may have not. But she certainly did not make me a better person, and people still knew me! And at seventeen or even twenty, that was what mattered. I cannot bring myself to ever say my final goodbye because even when I had left her, I knew she would still be alive somewhere out there. Because saying my final goodbye would have meant that everyone who had even slightly cared for me was gone; that I was truly alone in this world.

But the thing is, being alone is very different from being lonely. And I had never felt lonely after I had left her, so why would I feel it now? There was no point in looking back at my past if I was not even learning from it. I couldn't remember the last time I had written something. I had vowed to never be weak, and yet the glue I had used to put myself back together had dried up with each memory about the age of fifteen and then seventeen and then thirty; and now I was halfway broken. I was disappointed in myself. I did not care, I had to move on.

It was my thirty-second birthday, and I needed closure. That night, I visited her grave. I hung around for an hour. I wanted to talk but the words were stuck inside my body. So, I sat there in silence; it was unusually comforting. I heard the crunching of leaves; someone else was visiting the graveyard as well. I knew I had stayed for far too long. I went back home and sat at my desk—something I had not done in weeks. I took out my pen, and the ink took to the page. I didn't stop until my eyes were half-closed. I don't know if going to her grave has helped. But the thing is, I'm on the other side of the door and she cannot open it anymore.

Listen to the Tone (Watching The Cinema In Bed)

I'm sitting on a barstool, at a party full of people I don't know, even though it feels like I'm the one who is nameless. Nothing here seems welcoming, so I go to the place where everyone will judge me equally: the middle of the dance floor. It's funny; I hate being in front of everyone yet it's the only thing I seek when I walk into a room. It's been ten minutes, twenty or maybe an hour or two since I sought the middle of the room and right now, I'm dancing under a mirrorball. I see someone walk across. I don't have to look back to know it's my friend Ray. Well, not my friend *per se*, just someone who I'm sure will leave me the moment I take a step away from *everything*. I don't know why I look back but I do. Concern doesn't suit him, so I know that whatever expression of worry he is wearing is fake. It's mocking, it's glaring, but it's fine.

I think he grabs my arm, but I'm not sure. I think he drags me across the floor, but I'm not sure. I think he pulls me out of the party and out of the building, but again I'm not sure. All I remember is him calling me a taxi. I remember protesting, though I'm not sure if it was a scream or a mumble. Or maybe I didn't say anything at all. But I do remember pushing him away. He's already hurt, so all he shows me is his fake expression of worry. I remember trying to tell him that I wanted to dance in the middle of the room, that I wanted people to look at me, that I wanted them to not see through me but see me as they saw fit. I guess my efforts are futile because the next thing I remember is sitting in the back of a taxi. The party carried on but the mirrorball was gone. I'm not an ordinary person destined for ordinary things. I'm me in a thousand different images, just that I don't recognize all of them. I'm the one dancing in the middle of the dance floor every day, pretending not to care every time they look. That can't be ordinary, can it?

I'm filtering through the pictures clicked by Ray. *A mirrorball hanging. A mirrorball shattered on the floor. A girl on the dance floor; I don't recognize her. The same girl, drunk, on the barstool. There's me at the centre of the dance floor packed with people. There's me again, on an empty dance floor.*

I've lost track of the people that have come and gone in my life. Just blurred faces, dancing on the floor, until the lights have come on.

Ray calls me. I don't want to answer, but I do. I don't want to smile through the call, but I do. I don't want to ask him how he has been in the last few hours since I saw him, but I do. If he senses something amiss, he doesn't ask. I sense he's at another party, but I say nothing.

How an hour can change you. An hour ago, I felt like the best I would ever be and now I'm picking myself apart in conversations I don't even remember. I don't know how to function without the public. Maybe that's why I'm friends with Ray, even though I don't want to be. I don't know who I would be if I didn't mind people filtering out my broken pieces but keeping the parts they see fit. I don't know who I would be if I didn't cry later, sitting on the bathroom floor.

Ray clicks pictures of everyone, but mostly me. Maybe that's also a part of the reason I'm talking to him when I would rather smash the phone on the floor. I want to be seen through someone else's lens once in a while, but that doesn't mean that what they show is not what I am. I know where I come from. How I grew up watching movies in that one cinema in my town and now, I'm starring in them. Yet, the moment I step behind the camera, I'm everything other than myself.

Ray is a phenomenal photographer, that much is true. Really, an hour can change everything. I had my mask on, and now I'm me, in the mirror, but I don't recognize the person staring back. The same goes for his pictures; unedited, I see someone I don't recognize. But I instantly recognize the woman who emerges later in the edited pictures.

I sigh and look at the pictures again. My vision is glassy but I think it's just the dust in my eyes. My cheek feels wet to the touch but I think it's just sweat. There is no camera in the room;

I wipe my face and put on a smile. I would like to go back to my hometown for just a day. I would like to go back to that cinema and eat popcorn and pretend to be that little girl whose feet couldn't touch the ground. But I'm lying on the bed, my feet going past the bed frame thinking about how I hate popcorn these days.

Listen to the Hesitation (Waves Crashing Into Nothing)

She had always pretended that her fears were like a swimming pool. She'd always stand on the edge, looking down on everything that made her, *her*. And everything she was scared of. And she'd never venture deeper than the depth covered by a single toe dipping in the cold water. Perhaps it was the hostility of the temperature of the water or the emptiness in her mind at the thought of drowning; or perhaps it was the thought that she would find something about her she had buried in the deepest part of her mind that would change people's perceptions of her. This deep blue water seemed to hold her whole being as if she was only made up of her fears and nothing else. She had believed this ever since she was young, and it is very hard to let go of something that you've made your home. This edge, this water, this depth, it was daunting.

When she was young, the school took her class to the local swimming pool. She had almost drowned. The cool water burned in her throat and this sense of fear was something out of this world. It had felt like the end until a girl had dragged her up to the surface. She had promptly walked out of the pool and never went in again.

Listen, she had always been scared that she would never amount to anything. As if all that could be achieved in the world had already been achieved by someone else. And so, this swimming pool of fear threatened to drown her whole. And this sense of despair could never be told to someone else because it was almost embarrassing how she felt so hopeless in life when all people did, in the end, was die. So, she remained silent and the swimming pool first became a pond, then an ocean.

By thirty, these waves crashed into nothing but everything. If only she was a bit further away then she wouldn't hate the water, the friends who told her they were proud of her, and the parents who said she didn't have to be anything. Because the thing is, she did want to be something this world hadn't seen.

She never knew how to finish something, so this story was almost left unsaid. She changed every day and it was so exhausting. They didn't know how the words stuck in her throat, how she wished she could control it, how the waves crashed and she almost drowned. How the water scared her but she still built sandcastles near the water.

She had always pitied battered women until she realised a part of them was in herself. If only she could hold their dreams and know that even at their lowest they could still be themselves. If only she could hold their dreams and treat them as her own so that she could have the strength to continue. Because endurance had never been taught but always learnt by people who had oceans for fears and laughter for wounds. Let's run, she would tell them because there was strength in that, too. She had always pitied battered women until she realised she was one herself. And that, maybe, she would always be one.

Perhaps if she had thought about it more, she would not have been this scared. Like always assuming that she could only be one thing or the other and knowing that if she chose one thing, she would always regret never picking the other. Like people would always be wary of her and all she would ever do is sit at home screaming at all the people who were supposed to love her. But it never happened, so she stuck around in grocery store aisles and bookstore shelves because she was too scared to face the loneliness in her life.

She never got around to diving in the pool again; it was written in invisible ink. That she would always find it daunting, cold and hostile. And that she would always be standing on the swimming pool edge, knowing it was so much bigger than that. And maybe that was for the best. The waves crashed into everything and yet nothing.

Listen to the Desperation (Haunting Apologies)

I have a lot to apologise for. Even to myself. I have long given up on the idea of a perfect life. I am bothered by the idea of living for nothing—a reason to live that does not exist. I am also bothered by the idea of having too much money, thinking it is everything, and yet waking up every morning feeling sad. In that sense, both ideas consist of nothing. Having nothing and living because of nothing, and having everything but living because of nothing. I have a lot to apologise for.

It seems I always break whatever I touch; I've been doing it since I was two. Some people say I'm clumsy, but I'm not blaming myself for this reason. I am blaming myself because I am selfish. I had a friend, and I left her because she cared too much about other people. Looking at her made me want to look within and change. I apologise because I have always been so scared of change. I am not where I want to be. I look at my life and feel like crying. I am right where I belong because of all my efforts and actions. People say I have a tumultuous life, but I also have a tumultuous mind. Sometimes I really want to be understood, but I am scared of it as well. I apologise.

I say sorry too much; I apologise. My mother loved me too much; she was disappointed in who I became. I have killed and I have been killed. It seems I don't like it at all now, and it is true. I do not understand if I wander about like a ghost or if I'm looking at things from a movie screen. Death had intrigued me too much when I was young, and now I am dead. I am meant to haunt myself. I do not understand how it works. But I walk about the Earth seeing myself alive. Like a detached soul who could never find her way back.

I have made a lot of mistakes in my life but the worst one has been losing her. See, I always thought I had a reason for doing things and having an explainable reason for action would excuse the action itself. But, that's wrong. There are unexplainable reasons and then there are actions that do not have reasons—should not have any reasons—just consequences. I have always cared even though it never seemed so. I talked to a boy once; he thought I was mad. I've cried too much; it doesn't feel like it will ever stop. Sometimes, you become so used to people leaving and then coming back, that losing someone never hits until they actually go away.

I wish it was a dream; but it couldn't be called a dream because I have hurt people too much. If only I had paid attention to how she was hurting, I would have stayed longer. I'd get the tea that my mother only reserved for guests, and pour it. I have become a stranger to myself and to her. I blamed her so much for changing that I became blind to whoever I was becoming. I am dead, I know. I'm stuck, I know. Even though I know I'm here to look at myself, I am following in her footsteps. As if when I was alive, I never paid attention to her words and to her hurt; the hurt that now I cannot bear to look at. I wish I could hurt the same way I hurt her. That way I could understand her pain and all my mistakes. This is not to say that I do not understand them already; I just feel like I deserve it. Our story is still lodged in my throat, and it would be better if people grabbed it out of me. But then it would no longer be her story to tell, would it?

She gave me a lot of advice; I should have paid more attention, I'm sorry. I'm dead but I see myself as alive; this makes no sense. I wish I could have seen when I had changed so I could improve. I hate compliments now because it seems like each day, I hurt her one way or the other. She tells me that I pretend to be the victim; I never noticed but I guess it's true. Even when I found out I was walking on Earth dead, my first thought was who had wronged me.

I remember the first time we fought. I got a text and I thought it was her. I apologise. I'm still too hung up over it. I wish I could talk about my feelings without seeming to make everything about me. Because killing does not always mean murder. Why do we behave like this sometimes? Pretend not to care for their words but it kills us when they call us out. Doesn't that make everyone a murderer? I'm a murderer, too. I stand on that blood that dripped because sometimes your actions hurt more than your words and this time I have messed up royally.

I know I won't come back this time. This is the first time I have ever had someone burn because of me. This entire time, I thought she was the one doing it to herself but each word from my mouth is gasoline and each touch burns. She was right there, but a moment later she left. Why did I not notice? Or maybe I did and just made excuses. Sometimes apologies pile up and they start seeming fake. Is that what's happening now? Because, I swear, I do not mean it. I do not even know why I'm half dead and half alive, but I'm sorry. She is probably hurting even right now.

I mean it for real this time. If this feels like a trap, she should just tell me and I will let her leave in a heartbeat. I know it's important to understand who is hurting you and cut them out of your life. But it feels too far gone, and if she won't do it. I'll have to do it myself. The only thing I will ever say is for her to swing right at me and not miss. I told you; I want to hurt exactly the way I hurt her. It seems worthless now.

I know it's not real and she doesn't exist anymore. I'm all alone—a detached soul looking for something when everyone's left, looking for something in the emptiness of a person's being which was all because of me. I wish I could have danced with her one last time; I wish I could have said we could fix this without ever mentioning that it wasn't my fault, because it was. I wish I could reach out; I wish I had been killed without having killed. But sometimes, you don't always get what you want because you're selfish. And you don't always get what you want because you break things you touch. With every word said, you carry a knife. And for that, I apologise.

Listen to Who Lingers (Reflection)

I reach out to the girl in the mirror. I hold my hand out and she does the same. I am almost touching her but at the last moment, I turn away. She does, too. I'm confused. Why can't she have the strength to reach out? Or maybe she does and yet, she waits. For *my* strength and my hand. Maybe she always knew what was going to happen and still waited. Maybe she knew I would turn away and maybe she felt as if this was my story to tell, my time to reach out. Maybe she had done it years ago, and I hadn't been there to receive her. Or maybe she knew I wouldn't have come and yet had hoped.

That girl had disappeared years ago, and yet I saw her in my old group of friends or sitting at the back of the classroom or maybe talking animatedly while knowing no one was listening to her. She was a shadow, a grey apparition, and yet in my eyes, she would always be the burst of colour. I could never talk to her. I was scared and maybe it was because of the fact that I had hurt her so many times. Or maybe the fact that when I looked at her, all I could see was the sadness in her eyes. Her eyes glistened with tears that no one could see, or maybe saw and yet chose to think it was the light falling on her eyes.

I noticed something one day when I looked at her, barely standing at the brink of her supposed close circle of friends. She was grey and yet her eyes were deep brown, almost black, and sharp. She noticed everything—the way one friend would roll her eyes and others would look away when she talked. She noticed me the most. The way I'd look at her and know: she was strong and yet so weak. She had been my downfall. The hand faltering on the shoulders, the way they did not stop, the slowing of steps, and then the pause. The girl stood on the first step while they were already on top. I couldn't help but think it was because of me. As if I was a weight, the only thing holding her back. If I could just peel off her skin, would she still be me? If I could just show that the veins were still blue and red and she was just like them, would they still have said that they were purple as if I was someone other than human and that meant she was, too? If I could leave, would I go? Would I look in the mirror and tell the girl she could be someone else? Would she agree?

She lingered at every party and at every door she dared not enter. Like the whispers that followed her, she followed them. If they talked, she knew; but the face hides many things and I was right there. She was just like the group of friends. The difference was that she had done everything because she *had* to, but the others had done everything because they *wanted* to. She was the best of my life. I lost her. But I remember, I was right there when she screamed at them, hiding the younger girl. Her veins might have been purple but her face was red and her knuckles white.

I wanted to run away from the mirror; the past was something less than a sweet memory and I was half-broken. The other half of me was across the mirror—the girl that waved and waited. I was halfway through the door, and she lingered. She gave her blood, sweat and tears for this and yet why did it feel like I was still bleeding? I still have the drawings she left, her messy handwriting on diaries, and kindness that used to be overflowing.

I'm still at the mirror.

I'm half hurt and half fed up, like I'm gone but I can come back. Like I can reach out and she would not go away. Like I can think about giving up but still don't. Like I can say goodbye to the girl in the mirror and still remember her. I may be half of the person she is but that is not a bad thing. If I could I just look backwards for a minute, maybe I would see how far I've come, but the girl is the only remnant. I am taller now.

Listen to the Music in the Back (Arcade)

Have you ever gone to the arcade and simply watched people play? I need help when I go there, but no one knows. I am sure if I were to cry, it would come out as a voice crack, lost in the many sounds of the arcade. It is safe here, I hope. The shouts and the screams. I am no one but just a body in this crowd. It feels good here; in another world, it would not have.

It used to set me free all those years ago. When my mother saved up enough to bring me to the arcade because all the mothers were doing so, she would tell me to stay close by. But I was a child, and all those teenagers with their headphones were giant bodies. A place filled with all these big people would be constricting for someone as small as me. But I would be fine because I could see my mother's shoes through the gaps.

Today I am taller than those sixteen-year-olds, but I am still not free. Whenever I go to the arcade, I stick closer to the door, pretending she is still around. I am still so small. Even now I feel constricted when I see all these people letting go. This irony should make me laugh, but it only gets harder to breathe. I stay put, just like I should have done all those years ago. I get it now.

Do you know what happens when you try and try hard, and then you are seventeen, and high school begins to feel like a fever dream? You fade away. It is an unavoidable fear, I used to tell people. The brutality of this sentiment would scare them. At one point, it scared me, too.

I thought I was stronger than this. Livid, dreaming, hoping.

When all the people I could have called friends hated me, I thought it would pass. In the books, it always did. The main character would go through incidents of pain, but you knew that three-thirds into the book, things would be well. In life, I learned that sometimes the three-thirds of the book lasted for eight years. The thing is, I never did figure out why they hated me until I found out the reason why my own mother hated a part of me. This anger had passed down from her mother to her, and then she had passed it on to me, just like she should have passed on love. If only I could have been content with simply being seen, and had never been loud, desperate and livid.

There's an art in doing the most trivial things. Didn't you know? I am boring, I know. But it was an art. I have seen the same scenery being painted by a thousand people. And I will want to ask you over and over again: How is it that it was never the same? How can we marvel at the next one like we did at the previous one? This is a question I get to whisper in the safety of the arcade.

So, each time I went to the arcade, I would not just notice the same machines repeatedly, I would see different people. And when playing, it seemed as if they had someone they could go back to, in a way that I could never do. I do not mind being alone. I can still go to the cafe and order a pastry; I can still go to the amusement park and easily get into the single ride lines. But sometimes, I wish I was not so lonely.

Some days, I am taken back to the backrooms of the arcade when I was just on the brink of adulthood. You came up to me and I had talked to you so casually. At that time, I thought I was doing you a favour. Everyone loved me then, and no one knew who you were. Later, I knew I had messed up when I told you I wanted to be a writer and you told me all your secrets to make me spill mine. It was done and it was too late. I had to let you go. The only person I had was me. These days, friendships are beyond me, so I write about you.

I used to be brilliantly promising, didn't you know? They used to say I would do great things. I needed those words like I needed to breathe. Where did it all go wrong? It was the moment I was born a girl—a monstrosity, but also just a girl. When people tell me over and over again that it was all my fault, I remember that all people can do is keep coming back to the idea of a monster. A girl, a destroyer and just as destroyed. A pointing finger never leaves you, you know. My mother was screamed at because she did this and she did that. This dream is real and it repeats itself over and over again. A girl gets born, a girl dies and continues to die. Lonely, cold, livid.

I do not put up with their words anymore. I need someone to brush past me, touch my hair slightly so that I can believe I am real. I have questions; I will store them in my head. I will go to the cafe and I will go to the amusement park. I will change. I will cry myself to sleep but become stronger. I'm still the young girl my mother held.

I am over everyone now, three years later. I went to the arcade the other day. The game machines used to be so big; they were much taller than me. But now, I have to look down at all of the screens with the music, the noise, the laughter, and the time I could never spend playing.

I cannot be set free.

Listen to What Always Has Been (The Number In The Drawer)

I still have her number. I had told her I would call when we both would be in our respective colleges. But I have an apartment in New York now. The idea of talking to someone you would never see in hallways or cafeterias again seemed trivial back then. When I graduated from high school, I had a feeling I would never come back to that town. Each step away seemed like a new possibility and it had been a long time since I had felt that way; I wanted to chase the possibility. I chased it right to college, to a job, and then to New York.

When she had given me her number, I had thought she was crossing a line that would never be crossed again. It had felt like a formality; I thought she wanted to continue being friends. But chasing possibilities meant leaving behind whatever seemed trivial.

Lost chances are like a tragic book—even though you pick it up only once, it touches your heart and so you display it on your bookshelf forever. The sticky note on which I wrote down her new number is folded, the glue turning to a sickly black. Everyone has a drawer—a place where the past lies; I do not dare walk the boundary of everything that is back in time. I do stumble upon it sometimes because it is very hard to forget, but just so easy to remember. The thing is, I don't want to remember because every time I tell myself I am over all the pain I must have caused, it feels like a lie.

My entire life, I have been taught to throw away things that are just too mundane because what you want is much stronger than a person, a thing, or a friendship. Not calling her feels like a betrayal not because I want to be friends again—I know I lost that chance a long time ago—but because I never told her about what I had been taught. The sticky note is a reminder that it is okay to leave things behind, mourn them, and still feel like it was for the best. Mourning feels like the evening fog when you're walking home. It's overwhelming and sometimes all you wish for is a clear sky. I am happy. I got an apartment in New York, just like I told everyone I would. This mourning does not define me or how far I have come in life. Mourning is remembering your friend but never calling her. It is not a hindrance to what I want, so I guess I am fine with it but only if I sometimes don't let it control me. I want to be successful and that is all that matters to me right now.

Just like me, she too has a life somewhere. So I guess in a way it all worked out in the end. But let me just say that I know it is my fault. I didn't call or care that she gave me her number. I didn't even give her mine. In a way, I hope she's forgotten about it. I can just be her old friend from high school, or the person she shared her classes with. All I am saying is I don't care if I am a nobody to her now; I know I deserve it, and at the same time, it doesn't hurt me.

I still have her number and in all honesty, I wish I didn't. I am too set in my ways; I know it and I'm not delusional to know that the idea of having a friend never really meant anything to me. I am not sure where she is; I'm still in New York. I am not sure if she even went to college, not because she didn't tell me when we graduated but because I had not been paying attention. I had looked at the sky that day wondering if I could ever become who I wanted to be and if this town would ever come back to me. I am not her friend; I already have everything I need.

I have a feeling that she has already forgotten about me; after all, we haven't talked in years. High school was a different time altogether and that time has passed. I finally feel accomplished and I don't feel like going back to my town. I believe that leaving trivial things is so important. So, I didn't call her. I just wish she knows that some part of me is sorry.

In the beginning, I wanted to never touch the sticky note again. This time, I take the old sticky note out from the drawer while making sure I don't dwell on other items present in it. I am standing in my New York apartment knowing that I made it, and I sigh. I didn't know it would be this hard but I know I have to do this. This time, I tear the sticky note and drop its pieces in the bin.

Listen to What Has Been Lost (Life Through Small Moments)

I have always felt like I've been missing something in life. As if I will always be missing something. Like when you lock the door to your apartment and your coat feels too empty. Like you leave a piece of yourself at home and then take something from the grocery store that is not food.

Often, I would leave a part of me in the bathroom lights that I forgot to switch off or the music that kept on playing from the radio my parents gave me when I moved out. At times I would take something from an apology for bumping into an old man in the soup aisle. And I would still feel as if I were missing something; as if there was a hole inside me that would never fill. A hole that other people would gape at—something that would belong to them when I would hang out with my friends. They would own the hole for a day or two and then sell it to the pawnshop. Even though the hole would be theirs, it would all come back to me. As if this emptiness could only belong to me.

I was at the grocery store and I wandered up to the counter with nothing but gum in hand. The cashier asked me how I was; I said I was fine. She smiled and I smiled back. It felt like someone had grabbed and pulled my face to show the stretch of lips, the white of the teeth, and those tears of mine of which there was an ocean inside of me. I will always remember that moment; she probably won't.

I have known life for a far less time than the neighbour who waters his plants—while mine are all probably dead—and yet I feel like the only person I'll ever amount to being is this half-broken mess who still cries when the book ends. I'm sick of thinking that whatever action I take is the end; as if I can never grow; as if I'm already dead.

I walked outside for some miles for the first time in months; I was out of breath when I took my first step. I felt like a child learning to walk for the first time (I have always felt like a child). As if I'll always hold the sleeve of the sweater my friends are wearing when I'm walking through a crowd. As if I'll forget how to use a paper clip the next time I remember they exist. I walked, and my white shoes got dirty when I got too lost in my head. I forgot to put my headphones in; that's what I say when my male friends ask why I live in the sound of my loud breaths. But I never forget; I will always leave them at the kitchen counter the moment I remember that music means that I can die on the streets. I remember that to be a woman is to fear every step you take outside your apartment—fear your neighbour, and fear the sleep that takes you every night because that makes you less aware, less dangerous, and less human for the person who breaks in.

I'm missing the person I'll never be more than the person I was when I didn't have to fake a smile. I read a book sitting on the fire escape, not because I love the smell of the hotdogs being served in the food truck right below but because I wanted to look at the sky for a minute and realise there was more to life than just looking at boxes, more to life than the box I had made for myself. It's harder to get out than it is to get in. I bought the apartment and now it's hard to venture outside because I have everything inside.

If I'm saying sorry, I know I better mean it. But these days, it's hard to mean something. I visited the library on a Monday when I should probably have been working; I was feeling spontaneous. I wanted to read fifty books this year; I didn't mean it. I said sorry to the woman who probably waited a long time for me to get to the door she had held. It spilled out of my mouth, like water but so bitter. I said sorry because my mouth knew that word; I just never knew how to feel it. No one had ever said sorry to me in a way that told me that they had meant it, and I went on living like no one ever would. It's hard to unlearn something—like I'll always say 'yes' in my mother tongue even though I live in a world where people just prefer 'yes'. It's hard to unlearn, because I had to force myself to cover my mouth when I would be on a call with my mother. I would say 'yes' in public, look up for a second, and be relieved when I wouldn't feel the hardness in the eyes that would glance at me.

My throat always held a rock the moment I would try to speak. I would feel the roughness, and I would realise again and again it was hard to swallow. I would look in the mirror because I thought it would make things easier. But my voice would shake and my lip would quiver and my hands would wobble. I hate to admit it but it's always been like that. I can't blame it on the cold for the trembling, or the rock for the difficulty in swallowing; I just have to blame myself.

I walk alone in the winter but I feel like everyone knows me in the city because wherever I go, I have to mess things up. Like the family that lives near the mall knows I broke one of their plates; the old woman who watches the dogs in the park knows I tripped over nothing. And it's probably nothing, but why does it feel like people rarely forget and forgive even less. I don't want to wear the bracelet I wore when I was fifteen because I'll only see the things I'm missing; the thinness of my body, the fullness of my soul, the sound in my laugh, and that I knew more back then, than I know now.

I've collected broken promises when I should have collected seashells. I decorate them on the walls of my apartment so that everywhere I look, I feel sad—because that's the only way I know how to fill the hole inside me. I look at each promise and realise that most of the promises I have collected were to me. And it would have been better if I had said that I had come to terms with every bad memory, but that would be a lie.

When things become final, I get scared. I can think about all the decisions I have to make and that is fine, but the moment I take the final step, I just want to run away. I realise that I'm out of breath. Listen to me; I am tired. I realise that I'll never know when things end and it breaks me because I spent this entire time searching for it. And I'll never know when I'll finish the chicken my mother made; it's been there for days. I'll never know when I'll ever stop running but it takes me some time to realise that it's fine because I started walking for miles again. I'll never know if I'll ever get my body back but it's fine because I have this hole, and first I need to spend time filling it with something else but sadness. I need to keep it with me because it's like the stuffed toy from twenty years ago and because after all this time, I need to learn. And when the morning comes, I know I will probably realise what a mess I am, but tonight, I'll hide underneath my blanket, the bedroom lights still switched on, my heart on a sleeve that no one will ever see, and cry even more.

Listen to What Has Been Let Go (Glass Half-Poured Down the Sink)

My current predicament with glasses of water started with a glass half-full. I had turned eight the day before, and was feeling older and better about myself. Sitting high atop someone's shoulders had felt like the farthest a human could ever reach. We had new neighbours and I had found out there was a kid across the street, so I made it my mission to be friends with him. So there I was, freshly eight, in the kitchen, and talking about the deepest topic I had ever talked about—a glass of water. He showed me the glass and asked me what it was. Even at that age, with my keen sense of observation, I knew that the new kid across the road was being very stupid. I looked at him and he went on to explain how if I had said half-full, it would have meant that I was optimistic, and if I had said half-empty, I was a very negative person. Of course, this conversation took place in simple language because the new kid across the road (who is no longer 'new' but a twenty-something gamer who spends his nights in his mom's basement) was quite stupid and had thought me to be a kid. I had thought I wasn't, though; I was eight and I had reached the highest height possible. So, I had said that it was half-full because he thought that it was the only correct answer. Also, everyone always had to be positive so I thought that, too. Over the years, he always told me to be positive over and over again and I did; I think. But, he's now in his mom's basement playing video games and eating salty crackers, while I'm standing in a new apartment, with the whisper 'it's half-empty' always on my lips.

As I look around the empty apartment, standing in a bare kitchen with no eighth birthday party leftovers and constant reminders to stay positive, I'm reminded of how far I've come. The new kid across the street who I'm no longer in contact with would laugh if he saw me here. I would, too. I fill up a glass of water to get rid of the bitter taste in my mouth. This moment is cut short (thankfully, contemplation is exhausting especially when I think about him) and I get a call from my office. This time, I take the elevator to the fifty-first floor of my office building and being on someone's shoulders is no longer the highest place I've ever been to. But, as I walk down the hallway to finish whatever business I had been called for, the glasses of water on the tables have a bittersweet effect on me. I take a deep breath and half-an-hour later, I'm done. I check the time and I'm sure that guy in his mom's basement is probably starting to set up his gaming set now and getting his daily pack of salty crackers. I'm done here.

I come back home and I walk into the kitchen to find a glass half-empty. I had forgotten to keep the glass in the sink. I'm suddenly reminded of my eighth birthday and salty crackers and false positivity and that new (now old) neighbourhood kid. 'It's half-empty' stays on my lips. I can't get rid of it.

A glass half-empty. A glass half-full. A glass of water.

It's fine now; it's all poured down the sink.

Listen to the Gaps in Between (Silence)

The room is dimly lit; two shadows paint the wall. All is calm and quiet, but if you were to walk into the room, you would feel uneasy. As if it is better to hang near the door for a minute or two than to come inside and pay attention. As if it is better to not make conversation with the people in the room because all you would hear is this overwhelming fear of failure. So, stay away. It is for the better. Yet, another faint shadow lines up. It stays.

The newest shadow asks, 'Are you ready?'

The walls echo, and the room is engulfed in this question. There is quiet anticipation and the third shadow sighs. It was naive to think the two sitting shadows would talk. The room remains silent but a minute later, the music is the response.

It slowly picks up pace, and becomes deafening. Two sounds intertwine like two elements: land and water. One cannot be without the other; it would lead to death. The sounds dance together. One is deep and rough, the other shrill and smooth. Alone, they would hurt the ears, make you hold yourself, but then make you want to run away from the despair of it all. But together, they bring life. The sounds dance smoothly together unlike the two making it. Their faces showcase determination and no kindness, trying to make sure the other remains defeated. The music stops for a beat or two as if they are taking a break. As if the silence wonders if there is a slight chance of reconciliation. Naivety seems like a curse in this room, although it remains unspoken. The third shadow is confused, almost wishing to speak in the silence.

But then, the music picks up, as if knowing the severity of the situation. Only one of them can be chosen. Their lives have been lived like a competition, always trying to beat the other because the embarrassment is too much to bear. And this is the final chance. To play for the queen, is to make your career for life. Money is not the reward they want. It is reputation. Reputation is easily bargainable but only if you have the power to do so. The queen knows and so do they.

There is a certain desperation that can be heard; the two players share a look. Contempt. Ambition. The third shadow notices, a faint smile on his face as if he knew all along this would happen. They have been competing for so long that this is the end. And, yes, with each note, their past flashes before them. It's almost a sad affair, to be honest. Knowing that this will be the last time they compete, because the next time they see each other, they will no longer be equal. And this sadness can be felt because music is not what you feel when you first compose it. Rather, it is about how you feel at the exact moment you're playing it. This sadness is like a secret language only they know about; they are almost too scared to continue, as if no one could ever know this grief. The music stops for a beat again. This feels like a mistake. Sadness. Contempt. Ambition. The walls seem to know. But the silence hides it all.

It picks up for the final time. This opportunity is too good to be passed, and so they know, no one is stopping for the other. Their lives have been destined for this moment, as if they were born to play this music, break and be pieced together, but knowing the entire time that the pieces can never fit. As if they were born to win and lose but would never know which one of the two it would be until this exact moment. Water and land coexist. But they cannot.

Listen to the Silence (Madame: She's Around The Corner)

She's collecting information like one collects seashells. She whispers on the beach; the crash of the waves engulfs her words and the mist envelops her.

Madame had a sad childhood. When she wrote, she never started her sentences with 'I'. She never waited for life to come and give her a push. When push came to shove, she did it all by herself.

—

Madame feels broken. Inspirational quotes in the newspapers break her even more. The town she lives in is similar to the town she lived in before. Her need for patterns has rooted her through each wave on the beach. That's why she doesn't run when the mist gets in her eyes. She had a lover, but the mind caged her before she could secure the ring. So, she said 'no' when he went down on one knee. She never had it in her to bear a child. No one could put that feeling in her. Or take it out. She had rosy cheeks when she came into the world. Now, she has rosy cheeks when she's caught around the corner, collecting information.

—

Madame always wanted to learn how to waltz, but never with a man. And so, feeble steps on the beach end up being washed away with the waves and a fallen woman laughing quietly. She's around the corner, listening to two old women talking about the bride that ran away before her wedding. The groom sat on the church steps and wept. She was around the corner, quietly reaching out to the bride in her mind. I understand you, she imagined herself saying. She could run and hug the bride. But the bride had run away; she didn't have the guts, the two old women whispered. Little girl, she doesn't understand this world, they said.

—

Madame has had her dress caught in all the runaway sand. The beach is crowded but the ocean looks lonely. If only she learnt how to swim. She hadn't learnt a lot of things. Like how being caught eavesdropping once meant it could happen twice. And so, with rosy cheeks, her eyes look at the huge cracks in the pavement. The local government should really come and examine those cracks once. And the old women really shouldn't have whispered that loudly; it's as if they wanted someone to overhear them.

—

Madame: it's her last day on the beach. Her last day ever. Her last conversation. Her last seashell. Her last waltz. Her last breath. She's on the beach; it's evening and the people start leaving. She falls, and no one sees. There's a sharp pain in her chest. She closes her eyes; she realises. She wouldn't go to the hospital even if someone tried. And so, she's lying on the beach, with her eyes closed.

—

She never got the courage to write something beginning with 'I'. Her last waltz was clumsy. The mist still engulfed her. And so the people leave, and a man walks past. His foot slightly touches her outstretched hand. So, he tips his hat and proceeds to say in acknowledgement:

'Madame'.

—

The man is gone with the last rays of the sun. Madame: she doesn't move.

Listen to the Punch (The Blood Affair At The Corn Maze)

She meets me at the corn maze on Halloween; I am already halfway through. As she grabs my hand, I drop it. I'm sorry, I want to say, but I don't; it's always been like this. The corn maze on Halloween night is the farthest I've been to feeling scared, but now that she is here, I am falling apart.

I continue walking and I know I'm being followed; she's behind me. She never understood social cues or the fact that I tensed up every time she was here. But, I also can't blame her for everything. I'm not perfect either. That's what stops me from screaming at her. That's why I let her follow me.

It's silent but it's too loud. I hear my thoughts and her sighs. She's such an imposter; she's cruel. I drop her hand and continue walking.

I'm at the centre of the corn maze now. I don't know what's in the middle; I can't see. She's standing in front of me, under the night sky; it's a painting of obsession. She whispers something, I want to run. But she might have more fun that way, so I stay. Tonight, I'm living in darkness and standing in a corn maze full of strangers dressed up for the thrill and the only thing I can find scary is the person standing in front of me. When we were young, she had decided that she adored the full moon while I loved the amber skies. When we were young and I would play with the kid across the street, she'd made him trip and had smiled at the childish thrill of it all. The blood from the kid's nose would fall on the ground in periodic drops, and I would stand in horror and watch her laugh. When we were fifteen, a year ago, I had come second in a competition. So, she had hurt the winner in a room I don't remember being in. Perhaps that's why I don't remember what had happened to the winner. She had told me later that the girl with the bigger award had been dealt with.

I'm at the centre of the corn maze now; she's in front of me and she repeats her words because I don't hear her the first time. She wants me to talk to her. I don't want to. This is only so far as I will allow our friendship to go. She calls me a coward for never talking to her and I call her a liar, because all she does is lie to herself. It's a full moon night and it feels like the end. Maybe it is. I can feel a fight brewing but this time, I don't do anything to stop it. She tells me that I'll never go far in life if I'm not impulsive, and I tell her I'm impulsive but not when it comes to decisions I think are bad. I may not mean it but I'm alone with a girl who comes and goes throughout my life.

She lunges at me at the same time I do. I punch her hard; I feel a sharp pain in my arm and in my head. I punch her stomach and then her nose. I'm crying and she is, too, and I'm feeling alive and she looks dead. The pain comes in waves, flows and ebbs. I see her lying on the ground with her eyes open. The corn maze walls stand formidable while I'm crumbling and falling. I feel something wet on my face as I watch the body on the floor with blood from her nose coating her lips.

I'm touching the blood on my face and dying to live. The blood quickly coats my lips. I smile as it dawns on me that I'm just like the girl whose hand I dropped in the corn maze on Halloween. The thought is so scandalous and sudden and there's an ecstasy about falling to the ground. I wish there were amber skies but it's just the full moon. I'm bloody and I'm her, and I'm red; tonight it's the death of me.

Listen to the Lies Lost (Mundane Thoughts At The Gas Station)

It was nine in the morning and he'd dropped his kids off at school. They had murmured their goodbyes and he'd been feeling okay; he just didn't know what to say to them. He felt sorry for himself and for his wife. Just then, he'd gotten a text. He went to that spot where they all usually met—his friends, or perhaps they were just people who made fun of him and his stupid pickup truck. But that was not a problem; he was always fine because he was Jason—he was himself, and for those couple of hours, he was the centre of attention.

Now it was seven in the evening. Jason was in *the* car, with a band of thieves or people like that. He kept quiet. They were driving way past the speed limit and they desperately needed gas, but Raya drove on. There were five of them and Raya only caved in when the other three screamed at her and then at Jason for not making her listen. Those three always screamed, so it was fine, but this time they needed gas. Desperately. Raya drove slowly now and took the exit.

A couple of minutes passed before they saw a small gas station. They wouldn't have even noticed it but the sign had caught Jason's eye. Buy gas for $20 and get free coffee for all. When he showed them the sign, those three laughed. They always laughed at him. Who needed coffee from a sketchy gas station? But Raya did, so they stopped.

Raya paid for the gas and they were ready to go. But where was the coffee? Those three wanted coffee now. It was a boring sunset, not so red or orange. Just yellow and light blue. They needed coffee to survive the night. Jason liked the sunset, and Raya thought that the sunset was pretty. But those three didn't, and they needed coffee. Raya did, too, and wanted them to wait for Jason and her, but they had already gone into the shop.

It was a boring sunset and the smell of gas was like poison, but Jason could do with it just to have this moment. To sit in the passenger seat and to listen to those three scream, and to see that Raya was disgusted. At everything, especially him. But Jason was as fine as one could be in the company of thieves looking at him as if he were something alien. He was fine; he was himself. He was hated, and he hated his family life. So, he was here with Raya and those other three stopping for coffee, wondering if life could get any better. Or any worse. He left her in the car and went in to get the coffee just because he needed something to do.

The small shop was run-down, like the gas station, and the screams of those three could be heard even inside the shop. Jason had walked away from Raya slowly, as if he wanted Raya to stop him and apologise. But for what, he had no idea. Apologise for his life, perhaps. Raya and those other three had laughed when he had told them he had two kids. They had laughed even harder when he told them he and his wife used to have weekly dinners with his wife's grandparents. So, he guessed he wanted them to apologise for his life. As he crossed the pumps, Jason picked up the pace and went straight inside to the coffee.

He could smell something different in the air, like something unnatural; maybe it was the cheap oil in the popcorn machine. Those three were screaming again and the man behind the counter was smiling weirdly. His two bottom teeth were missing and he had shaggy blonde hair, and dark circles under his eyes. But who was Jason to judge? He wasn't going to take the moral high ground even though he thought he was constantly being judged by Raya and those three. He wasn't going to judge because he was here for coffee and a getaway. So what if a raggedy gas station employee was now part of his getaway, all he had to do was to look past and find coffee.

It was a mundane life, dropping his kids off at school. It was more mundane now to care too much for coffee. It wasn't just about coffee, though; it was about not being with his wife. He didn't mind getting free coffee in the last hours of the day as long as it was another fifteen minutes away from his other life.

By the time he had taken his free mug of coffee from the shelf, Raya had caught up and had started doing the same. Those three were silent now and that was unusual. Raya had frozen now, just like Jason. Those three had hazy looks on their faces, and that was unnerving.

One of them whispered, 'We shouldn't have come here. We shouldn't have.' All three of them fell like dominoes in succession. This night was certainly full of surprises, Jason thought. He didn't want this; instead, he wanted familiarity in the chaos. And right now, the three were silent. Jason's voice shook as he asked Raya if they were going to do something about it. Raya seemed to come back to life now and shook her head. She believed it was one of their pranks, and told Jason to just forget about it. They were probably laughing silently.

Jason looked unsure, but Raya seemed determined to enjoy her coffee. Jason took a deep breath and looked back at the gas station employee. The employee smiled unnaturally and told them from across the shop to just call if they needed anything.

Raya immediately mentioned that the coffee was almost finished and that the employee would have to fill it up again. He told her that she would not get another free cup, and that if she wanted something, she would have to pay in cash. The gas station employee kept on smiling but there was a hint of annoyance in his voice as if he was in a hurry. For someone in an empty, run-down gas station shop, which Jason guessed got two customers per day, the gas station employee acted as if he was a powerful being.

A couple of minutes passed before Jason finally gave in to the urge to make sure those three were alright. So, he bent down, ignoring their wide eyes, and checked their pulses. This was how

Jason realised they were dead, in a run-down gas station, under a boring sunset. Jason was beside himself, frozen with shock, while Raya sipped on her coffee slowly.

His eyesight was blurry; it must have been the dust in the air. His hands were shaking, maybe because the coffee was hot. They were dead, Raya found out seconds later. Her voice did not tremble as she asked him if his coffee was good. He didn't say anything and death took those three away to somewhere closer to the end of everything. Their eyes were still wide open and Jason just thought about how mundane it had all been. If goodbyes had been this easy, he would have dropped his kids off at school every day. But, no. That's why his wife dropped their kids off three times a week while he only did it twice a week. Because he had no idea what to say.

He had always chased that sense of belonging he had seen with families on the sidewalk and friends in the classroom. And so, yes, it did hurt a bit, but just a bit. Those three had died and with them died something intangible, indescribable. He did not like the feeling; he felt better when he understood that he had no name for it. If Raya was upset, she didn't show it. She didn't even seem confused.

They died from drinking coffee; that sounded so stupid. What if he died right now, at this moment? He let out a breathy laugh. Raya looked at him, confused.

Inevitability was life's greatest ironies, Jason believed. People were told to make their own decisions and forge their own paths; what they did and spoke influenced where they ended up. Yet, no matter where they ended up—in the bed, married and happy, or in a gas station, thinking about coffee—they ended in the same way as everyone else: dead. And so, an argument began between Jason and Raya, both of them dancing on the edge of death. If asked five minutes later about how the argument had started, Jason would have probably said he did not remember while Raya would point fingers at Jason.

And so, they fought about death, and then coffee, and then the gas prices but in the end, they felt woozy as if under a spell. Raya fell and then fell Jason.

'You'll never be free,' Raya spoke her last words. It seemed as if she'd been wanting to say those words for a very long time. Jason never figured out Raya and what her words sometimes meant; he would never know because he couldn't ask her now. She died with the last rays of sun streaming through the window. The gas station employee was nowhere to be seen but it was probably because Jason was lying face down on the floor thinking about questions that could not be answered because it was too late. Raya had said he would never be free, but she was wrong. Now that he knew he would die, he had never felt more free.

His whole life he had wanted to be free. For a while, he thought marrying would make him free from his parent's expectations. Then he thought that having kids would free him from his wife's expectations. When he had first started his getaways with the band of thieves, he had felt weighed down by their expectations, but over the months he had realised something. He was tied down by his own expectations. The realisation should have been freeing, but it wasn't. Freedom could not be found at weekly dinners with his wife's grandparents; could not be found at the bottom of the bottle at midnight, or even at weekly getaways. He found freedom on the floor of the gas station, cheap oil in the air, and the prospect of falling asleep and never waking up.

The gas station employee was now standing above Jason's body, and Jason could picture in his mind the employee smiling, some of his teeth missing, wearing a t-shirt with five holes. Jason realised the unnatural smell in the shop was definitely something supernatural; it felt like Jason's situation was being shown in a cinema because the supernatural only existed in the movies. Jason pretended to cry as if he was on camera for the last time. He looked away, shifting his body away from everybody.

It was nine at night, and he should have thought about his kids or perhaps his wife. He should have wondered what could have happened if he had said something to his kids when he had dropped them off. He should have wondered about his life, but, no. He just wondered about death, how weird the word 'mundane' sounded, and how the coffee had tasted a bit bitter in the last hour of his last getaway.

Listen to the Truths Found (Home)

Home

noun

1. the place where one lives permanently, especially as a member of a family or household.

As in:

Somewhere in my past, it is spring. The sweltering heat makes me want to go home, but I do not know what home is anymore. People walk past, all rushing to the nearest cool spot while I stand. The reality of this sinks in. This home was never permanent until it stopped feeling like a home. I stand on the sidewalk, almost oblivious to the crowds. I look up at the sky wondering where everyone was from.

At six, the home was the orchard behind the neighbourhood. Then home became my apartment complex. Next, home became the smell of oranges on my hand and friends at school. Home was then the touch of my brother's hand in the house in the suburbs. Until it all finally burned right to the ground. I had not been home and I had not realised that this was how quickly things could go. Home had been nothing constant and a part of me resented that because home was supposed to be something I could come back to. Home. It was orchards, oranges and skyscrapers until it became nothing at all.

I have hated all things temporary, like the breath that will leave me and never come back. When I was young, I thought I saw a star moving. My older brother told me it was just a satellite but I had already made my wish. I could not help but think about all the other times I saw satellites and wished and hoped before someone told me I was wrong. I never knew that stability was the thing most people chased until it was eighth grade and everyone was waiting to go to high school. I have hated all things temporary and I know life is the most temporary thing of all. It's a shame that we die. That he died. My brother always wanted to leave his mark on the world while I never cared. Sometimes, it felt like I would never be seen, even in death. Like I would quietly pass by. But now all his dreams chase after me and home still doesn't feel near.

School was supposed to be the next best thing. It hurt to live vicariously through all the hugs and the idea that other children knew which bed they would be sleeping in that night and the next. It hurt, but I needed it so I could drown in sorrow rather than regret. Anything but regret. Because with regret, I drown myself in what I could have done. It is a feeling indescribable but it eats at you from the pit of your stomach and it is so powerful that all you can think is that you could have done something. Why does regret leave you feeling like this—calling out for more just because you feel the need to scold yourself? Could anything comfort me when this feeling leaves goosebumps on my skin? Would it stop making me feel chaotic or is it just my mind? It drowns me until I cannot breathe and then suddenly I can. It comes and goes. So, sorrow is better than regret, especially in school which was supposed to be the next best thing.

I cannot stop people from judging, I know. But you do not understand. It was never supposed to be this way. I thought friends could not change, but I was wrong. I thought friends were alright but it's so much worse than that. She was the worst of them all. She sat in the back of the class and all the boys loved her; it got to her head. I did not understand but she pushed me; she screamed in my face. I was too frozen to understand what she said. I wish I had ridden my bike like a little kid who is not scared of the roads. Instead, I would rather hide in the hallway pretending I am in the bathroom. Because reputation matters to me and I wished on a satellite that I needed the strength to stay. That was before I knew satellites were different from stars the same way that I am different from the rest of the people in my class. I hid in the hallway; they must have called out my name. The day I graduated, I got away from this town that never really belonged to me. When I moved there with a new family, they said this would be home but they were allergic to oranges and then I ran away.

Home burned down to the ground a few years back and I didn't know what people meant when they asked me where I was from. I got a job somewhere doing something. It didn't matter to me what I did; I just knew I had to be the best at it because my brother always wanted it. I called her already, in case you were wondering. She said she wasn't sorry; I expected it. That spring, the only thing I wondered was how a person could resort to this. This hurt I knew for so long, and all for what? The reasons, I could never understand. How could someone resort to this; this was my life. This was who I was. Who was she to take it all from me? I called her and I regretted it. I wanted her apology but I knew she would not apologise. I can pretend that I do not think about her. Think about reasons, think about the fact life wasn't too kind. Think about how I feel like life would never be kind.

Home. Each day it seems I'm asking for something else. Most days I don't even know what I want. Because this spring, the extra sense of loneliness made me realise that the home that I had even before wasn't even a home. Home wasn't something unpredictable; it didn't make you wonder if you would come home to joy or to hurt. But, it was familiar, and in a sense, I thought this familiarity did provide some stability in my life. My older brother told me why when we looked at the sky, we were looking at the past and that thought always unnerved me. As if we would never know what the universe looks like in our present until years later. Just as people make mistakes and are too proud to admit to them, until years later. I felt this because I never wanted to miss out on anything, especially on possibility. My brother taught me to never talk to strangers, and that was fine because I never felt like talking anyway. But I was also not a good listener. I just quietly let things flow before people realised I was a force.

—

It is spring and I feel like I have been stuck on the sidewalk even though it has probably been five minutes. The sun seems to be settling down now and the crowds are thickening. I see a family come out of a bakery—mother, father, sister and brother. And all I can think about is it could have been me. Sometimes, these thoughts just overflow and it's shocking because I have spent my entire life telling myself it will always be futile; it will always be the same. Most of the time, I have these feelings for breakfast, coated on Sunday toast. I have water in between bites so I can fully stomach those facts. Without my brother, I do not know what to do because he told me to be this and do that, and as a five-year-old, I thought his words were a general truth. The thing is, sometimes it's hard to come out of that part of my mind that keeps reminding me I'm now an only child with no family.

I can't be the only one who thinks that this cannot be the end. This time has passed in loneliness because I thought by the time I would be thirty, there would be a home for me. But it did not happen, and in passing I heard people talk about how friends had already made their lives. I was scared that there were none left for me. It felt like the end. Until it wasn't.

I met a girl, somewhere, in another spring in my past. And when we met, for once, I stopped thinking about how things eventually come to an end; but it felt too good to be true. A few months later, we went down to the beach and as the sun set, I stared off into the distance and talked about the fires. I talked about this fire burning inside me—how I wanted to achieve everything there was to achieve for someone. I talked about the fires in my mind that threatened to make me go mad. And finally, I talked about my parents who were nothing more than names; I also talked about my brother. I talked about the fire that took them and how I blamed myself for it. I talked about how sometimes in my dreams, I heard their screams and how I could feel the fire. I talked about the sunset, and how everything felt bright red, and up in flames. I didn't know I had started crying, so she gave me a tissue and then told me about me.

Home

noun

1. the place where one lives permanently, especially as a member of a family or household.

As in:

Somewhere in my future, it will be spring. I will stop remembering that all things are temporary because living will be easier then. You will tell me that you will believe in me until I believe in myself. The sun will shine brightly and I will stop looking at it just to spite the happiness I feel.

The home I forever sought will never be with me. Somewhere, I will find peace in that fact.

Listen to What Hides Underneath (Patterns)

All my life, I have been finding patterns.

The carpet near the TV had little men all over it but no one noticed. The sweater has owls in its design but no one looked close enough. The eyes spoke for themselves, and it was futile trying to hide them. The sighs spoke a lot in the silence when there was a person someone hated. All my life, I have been finding patterns. It was such a tragedy that I never got to understand when someone started dying.

For over three years, I lived with a girl who was a mystery. Yet, there was something familiar about her as well. My roommate always stacked all her dishes from the previous day, at noon. We would always start talking in the evening like old friends but in the morning, it would be different, as if we had overstepped this time. By the afternoon, as she walked into the kitchen, I would want to talk but something would hold me back. This was my favourite way of going about my daily schedule. Even now, I drink my coffee and don't leave the cup in the kitchen until after 12. I noticed this pattern a few months after deciding I wanted to live alone.

I always knew how a friendship ended. It was always in the eyes. They would say it all. This sudden shift in what used to be something so close—that I could just hug it and forget for a moment how quickly things go—was what destroyed me the most. It made me feel as if I was destined to break apart, over and over again. The betrayal, it was nothing new. And yet, this friendship that ended, a friendship that wasn't even a friendship, was the saddest of them all. Because in the end, it wasn't the sudden shift or betrayal that hurt the most; it was letting her go and knowing we both couldn't have done anything about it.

People come and go, and I have grown up understanding it is part of life. But I have always wondered if there is someone in your life that continues to stay in your life, at your best and your worst. I watched a movie when I was young; the main character died and I vowed never to watch a sad movie again. I would always make sure to read the plot before watching the movie, as if spoiling the ending was so much better than hurting in the movie theatre. But what happened with her—the roommate—was something of a dilemma. It would have been better if I had known how it would end. I would have known not to get closer. But then again, if I had known the end, would I still follow the patterns that she did? Would they still be a part of me?

My roommate died in the hospital—some sickness I never bothered knowing about. I felt this hurt like a knife, as if someone had stabbed me and twisted it so deep that I was scared it would never come out. I had felt like crying, but I didn't cry. I had felt like screaming, but I didn't scream. I carried on with my day, but at night I watched my sorrows come alive. The thing is you don't feel alone until you come back home and realise that the kitchen sink will only hold your dishes; the couch will seat only one person, and there will be no line that you will be too scared to cross.

There is something poetic about losing yourself when you lose someone else. It seems surreal knowing you will never hear the footsteps down the hall again, knowing that the face will only exist in pictures.

I moved out of the apartment soon after. I could see the patterns clear as day—the spiralling, the excessive sleeping, and the dishes piling in my room. I remember the day I found out she had died. Her mother called me. (I don't know how she got my phone number.) She said, 'My daughter has died.'

She didn't let me ask questions. She simply said her daughter had died, and then I heard a small sigh and then she hung up. That was that. As if it was just a fact and not an event that tore you apart. As if her daughter had died today but the mother had given up a long time ago. That day I lost myself. And so, I knew I had to get out of that apartment before this hurt inside me stuck around for the rest of myself. The thing is it never gets better; you just learn to live with it. There are nights in my one-room apartment when I reach the bedroom door and realise I cannot talk about the latest movie because she is not there anymore. I only knew how to cook for two people, the proportions committed to memory. How do I stop myself from reaching for two eggs when patterns can easily break but can never go away?

Dealing with death is like an open-ended story which one can look at in different ways. It never ends. Sometimes when people see a person dealing with grief quietly, they think this person has moved on because it is what they wish to see. Because knowing that grief ebbs and flows makes people think that you'll be drowning the entire time. If a child enters the ocean, the waves are the deep end, and the intensity is too much. But if a grown person walks into the ocean and the water reaches the knees, it doesn't mean the intensity of the ocean is any less; only that the person is taller. With grief, you just become the taller person, but sometimes there comes a larger wave that threatens to overthrow your security. The first thing you do isn't run; instead, you brace for the fall.

My mother made me go to a therapist. In the room, all I could think about was that this maturity couldn't help me. Over the weeks, we talked about death. She asked me if I was scared of death and I had to think about it because I struggled to explain this complexity of an emotion. Dealing with death, for me, is so much harder than the thought of me actually dying. I told her about a dream I had the night before. My roommate came back to me and I thought it was more of a nightmare than a dream. Some days, I don't even remember staring out the window wondering if I should call the mother or if she ever felt free from the past.

I didn't call the mother but I did ask the therapist. I zoned out before I heard the answer.

I always draw a line when I meet someone new. The line helps me remember I can't get hurt if I don't keep someone too close. I know I can't change all that I have felt in the past year, and a part of me does believe that this line may end up hurting me in the end, but I'm too tired. So, I created a new pattern, where when I get too tired, I know when to take a break. And when this hurt tries to talk to me again, I listen to music and watch the newest movie and think about how my roommate would have loved it because all the characters never got the courage to communicate their thoughts until it was too late. This line keeps the memory of my roommate safe, and I will always be scared to cross it like the nights when we were old friends and the mornings when we were like strangers in a restaurant sitting across the aisle.

My therapist told me to write all my feelings in a diary. I decided to write a story instead. I went to bed after writing the prologue. So, I know what will happen every day from now on. In the morning, I will make myself a cup of tea and sit on my balcony and open the black notebook. I will grab the pen but in my process of thinking about the past, I will leave ink stains all over my face. By afternoon, I will have written twenty sentences and cut out thirty more. In the evening, I will think about all my feelings and listen to sad music because I will feel like crying. At night, I will read each sentence, dry each page, and notice this pattern that will continue the next day.

I have always noticed patterns, and noticed how they can control what you do. I have always noticed pain—the friends that left and yet you still love them, the letters that were torn but later there was a struggle to put them back together…

It is a part of life…joy and sorrow. One can never be more than the other. And so, I hid this hurt but published the book. I hid everything that had made my roommate who she had been but never forgot.

She had died, and soon all it became was a fact.

Listen to the Fears (The Carnival in the Dead of the Night)

I visit the carnival each night. Sometimes willingly and sometimes unwillingly. But all that matters is that no matter where I start—whether in a sandy desert or a forest—I always end up at the same place. I've ventured here for years and I still haven't figured out why the lights stay on. The rides are so bright that everything hurts my eyes.

See, if it was a normal carnival, I would probably go with my friends. Except it's not. I would rather not venture there alone but it just happens. There are some things that will always be hard to explain; things I do not wish to explain. I have not known much except for the days I have lived and the carnival. It is an enigma shrouded in mystery and yet it feels somewhat familiar. Like when one is at the brink of a nightmare or maybe just before it ends. The thrill and fear are always similar feelings.

The photo booth is the bane of my existence. With every click of the camera, I'm further away from myself than I was the last time. The pictures come out of the slot, but it's never me. It's always the person I used to be. Younger, messier and shorter. I knew more then than I know now. As if I knew how they used me; I fail to see that now. The only reason I was sticking around in that town was because I was scared to leave.

See, there are moments in my life that I choose to forget during the day. Because in case I don't, I'll hesitate to continue; I'll have to pretend to laugh even when the blood rushes to my cheeks. I can only see all the things I wish I was, at night. My life has been great moments spread apart, sprinkled with stories that make me want to scream that I want to be more. More than this small body of failure. More than this voice that struggles to come out. More than the person who always listens. More than a simple existence. Be something so great that the sky shakes under this might; something so real that people don't forget this face.

Beyond the carnival is a place I do not venture to at all. The night is enveloping and suffocating, but the bridges make it worse. There is a certain air around the bridges that will probably take me someplace darker where I will be even more on edge. The bridges hold all the things I have hidden even from myself. Now all I do during the day is sit on the porch and watch the children play. It seems there are no secrets here. So, does it mean I was never really a child? Because I used to keep all these secrets that no one knew and I would stay at the carnival at night. Now, I'm too scared to stay. Not only on the outskirts of the carnival but anywhere really. I never had it in me to have the right thing to say; most times I just remained quiet.

The carnival is something familiar, and yet I don't want it to be. I have always wished I wasn't so worried; that I wouldn't lie and say that I was fine; that I wouldn't always think too much about the past. One thing my parents always taught me was to never stay stuck in the past. I don't know why I feel like I have failed. It is the one true thing I am best at. Failing. Falling. What's the difference?

I had a whole plan about what I wanted to do, but I don't anymore. I do not know why I cannot stop thinking about the carnival. My past is hidden behind this vivid facade and a part of me wishes it wasn't. I have to be good at something right away or I will always be thinking that the bridges are too hard to cross, the lights are always too bright and the carnival, a thing of dread. Maybe if I had known failure was something to be learned from, I would have crossed all bridges and would not have let them burn. We all have things we would have liked to learn from earlier, but maybe it wasn't meant to be. And so, I will continue to hate the fact that I have so much to learn.

I live in my mind during the day but hate the carnival at night. Either Audrey doesn't understand or she secretly knows what I'm talking about. She, too, has a fear of being understood. I've always been big on apologising to everyone but Audrey made me realise I never apologised to myself. I'm sorry I went to sleep but never slept. I'm sorry I've had many, many dreams without ever being asleep. I'm sorry the lights are still too bright even though it is dark. I'm sorry I'm too loud even though I am enveloped in silence. I'm sorry I'm like this. I'm sorry it's the dead of the night.

Listen to What Time Tells You (Diaries)

Diaries always destroyed me. Maybe because the emotional maturity I had been praised for, failed me when it came to personal matters. I have always battled with the idea of either being someone new or being someone unrecognisable. Because I know there is a difference. Because the idea of change seems like a beginning but all my past experiences tell me otherwise. Because I was left alone when I was someone new but I was loved when I was someone I did not recognize. I was loved in a way that made me want to run because I did not know what love felt like. Still, love should not have made me want to break all the mirrors in my house. And the diaries showed me someone I had met a long time ago. It seemed as if I only ever started living after I stopped writing in them, as if all the words I wrote in wobbly handwriting when I was seven, were written by someone that could never be me.

But it was, and that was what scared me. The fact that I had peaked when I was seven and that after everything that had happened, I was broken and I could never grow further. As if this was who I was meant to be for the rest of my life. I had a dream once; I was running and I was tired, but I could not stop even though I tried a lot. Even though it was a dream, I still woke up breathless. I would much rather call it a nightmare. I'm scared I'll never stop running. To put it simply, I am scared. Of my past. Of who I am now. And so, I have a lot of fears—that much is true—but the love I hold for things close to me threatens to overflow until I turn cold.

And the thing is that I love the person I was when I didn't care about what other people thought even though I rarely show it and talk about it even less. If I had loved her any less, I would not have been living in this agony. It would not have been a pit in my stomach that I could never overcome. And I would not have been living just so I could clench my heart because of the fact that some day, everyone would leave me. The thing is; it is an ever-persistent fear. As if it is the only thing that will never leave me; as if even when I am entirely stripped of my being, the only residue of who I used to be, is this fear. And I believe I would not have been living in this fear if I had not actually had it happen to me before. It was a sad affair because all that hope of them coming back, killed me. And each second chance I gave, meant I was going to get hurt all over again. And I know I should hate with my entirety, mean it when I say all those words, but part of me still misses them like a little kid. I wonder if I would come back running if they wanted me again, but then I remember how it was funny that everything shifted to nothing. It would make me feel a little less alive. And yet, I wish I could say with all that certainty that they didn't move me. But some nights are sleepless, and on some nights I wish that I didn't feel like a shadow.

There are days when this longing feels like a poem, and on other days it is like a knife going straight through my throat. I bleed through each part of my body and I wish I could befriend this longing, for that way I would come to terms with it. Because that would mean I will not wake up in the middle of the night remembering the fact that I used to eat my favourite snacks with my so-called friends who could probably earn money from the story about what a mess I used to be. On my better days, I pretend that that is not true. At my worst, I want to cry but I only just scream. And it is almost heartbreakingly poetic if I'm being honest. How I used to walk up the cobblestones with them and avoided all the cracks because when you're young, it could kill you. And now the only thing that kills me is the reminders of them, the snacks left untouched on the dinner table, and the fact I hated who I was with them. And still, I chase my old being, my old innocence, and still believe she deserved to be listened to.

After high school, I had no idea who I was. It felt like I would be coming back to square one my whole life. Some people spend their entire lives trying to win the race, and that is fine. And some people are already at the end, and that is fine, too. But what about the people who don't even get to start at the race because they're too busy trying to reach it. With each decision I make, it feels as if I'm destroying a part of myself. I wish I could go back to being the girl before I saw what the world actually was—not because she was naive, but because she was strong. I wish I had the courage, and that is the only thing I want in life. I never had a taste for white picket fences or the promotions I would get, moving from cubicle to cubicle. But courage? I am hungry for it; I need it. And sometimes, my self-control gets difficult; I am too impatient. I wish I could do something big, but that's fine; I know my limits. I know limits don't have to define you but there is absolutely nothing wrong with acknowledging them.

Sometimes I had the sudden urge to buy a new diary and start writing in it. I did buy the diaries but I would rarely write in them. What if my thoughts spoiled the pages, added unnecessary marks, made them unclean. I should have probably written that as well, but how was I supposed to put it down silently? And so the diaries piled up—reminders that I had failed somehow.

I have always wondered how one can define the feeling of failure. Is it a burning desire to do more and be more, or is it just molten sadness, too much at the same time? Is it that you feel like you can never show your face, never come back home?

So, diaries were all the failures I displayed in my room. I never wrote in them, and the blank pages felt like a waste. I never understood how people could express all their feelings on a random page when I would much rather hide them until it all overflowed. Some people felt at home within diaries, but not me.

The most at home I have ever felt is when I only think about being better, knowing I'll always fail. As if I were born to break that plate, that pen, that friendship. It's no good acknowledging it because, at one point in my life, I actually thought it would help me. But it didn't and it doesn't. I have always thought being the bigger person would take me somewhere in life. And lessons have been learned far too many times; all I'm left to do is think. I would have painted my life in gold, if I could. But it's cold where I live, and the snow has fallen for the third time this month; it's bleak and dark. And I all have is cheap aluminium foil wrapped around me; it barely keeps my emotions in check. The worst thing is, I would fall right back into who I was—someone I still hate and still love—just so I didn't have to keep finding myself over and over again and lie that everything will get better the next time I cry. And I have acknowledged, I am too broken to not hurt people. Every single person falls apart in front of me and I know it's because of me. I am probably not enough, but I am trying.

On some days, all you can do is miss. Miss the fact that you played with all your neighbourhood friends but now all you do is sit at home. Miss that playground you felt that you would always have happiness in the world and now you would rather not go there. Because that means you only have even more to lose.

I miss my past self; it's plain and simple. I miss when I did not used to be scared about the fact that I'll be lonely. And all my diaries would have echoed it back to me if I had been brave enough to write in them. I tried writing in them once, but if you'll see them now, all you'll find is the first few pages filled with my name and the last few pages full of drawings of flowers I probably hate now. As if there is only the beginning and the end and nothing in the middle. As if it is my life—my name is said over and over again when I was born—and then there are flowers on my grave when I die. I wonder if someone will ever visit my grave; if someone will wish I would never leave.

I would have called her a hundred times if I could just get an answer, even though I know most of the story. I'm halfway through my rage but still haven't had the time to process my sadness; it has always been like that. I know that I know better, but it feels like an obstacle I could never face. Who I used to be when I was seven is the best of them all, and who I am at twenty-seven is just someone made of holes—as if you can see where I was lost and where I am gone. You could see this anger if you looked hard enough; but the sadness? I know for a fact you would much rather see right through me.

I have spent a lot of my time trying to make sure people didn't feel the same sadness I did, and it was exhausting. Because a part of me knew I wouldn't be able to do everything to stop it. Life cannot always be happy, it is true. But some people don't have enough and that is what mattered to me. I tried confronting them once, and it was a disaster. I knew I was reading the chapters we had together over and over again, so much so that I had forgotten to read the rest of the book. Even though I knew that was what was missing, I never had the courage to read the rest of the book. For the fear that this pain would never leave, but the people would. For the fear that time would bring me back to this hurt again and again, just in different ways.

Time makes people forget and that is the greatest tragedy of them all. What about all the people I met when I was seven? What about all the moments that were never captured? And what about me? I am not who I was a year ago. How would I know how far I have come if I couldn't see it for myself? How should I believe in my family when I couldn't even believe in myself? And now, it seems time never really helped me at all. All I could see on their face was regret that the lie had to continue, and they never stopped. Time helped them forget about everything that went down but I didn't. Time wasn't on my side and it shouldn't be on anyone's for that matter, but it always felt like it was for them.

I wish I had had more time with the girl I used to be when I was seven. I remember, I had a citrus tree in my backyard and I would always want to eat the citrus fruit. But, I was too short and the only time I could eat the fruit was when there was someone tall enough with me. This entire time, I have waited to be the one who plucked the fruit without anyone's help. We moved out before I could. I think I have always chased the naivety I had when I was seven, not knowing the world could change in minutes and I would be left standing in the middle of it all, knowing the chaos, but never controlling it. I never knew that then but the thought kills me now. I wish I had more hope; I wish I could drink it as a glass of water every day so I wouldn't feel it seeping out of me with each breath. So I wouldn't feel like my time had been a waste.

There are situations when everything you have ever known comes crashing down. And the funny thing is, you cannot control it. I guess the thought becomes more liberating with each year that passes, but I remember the shock and the sadness when I first learnt that I would not be able to control everything. It felt like a betrayal. Whenever I had a conversation with someone, I would spend so much time making sure I wasn't making the conversation about me that I would forget that I was human too; that I could make mistakes. I could zone out and not hear what the other person was telling me and that was fine. I broke up a friendship when I left; she said I made everything about me. Even though I had spent my entire time making sure I had not. Even though I had loved each laugh that she laughed; even though she hated it; even though I knew that although I hated her, a part of me still loved her. I wish I could have written about it in a diary so I wouldn't carry this hurt like a memory. But some things are never meant to be, and that is fine, I guess. I still need to learn.

My thoughts have always been posed like a conversation in my mind. I witnessed my first snow the other day. The first half of me thought it looked beautiful; the second half wanted to see if the world would look the same after the snow had gone away or if the world was new in a sense. As if people in town knew it had snowed, but the evidence had gone away as if they carried it like an inside secret.

Do you remember shovelling out the snow early in the morning? Do you remember making hot chocolate for your family? And yes, the snow was gone, and the streets were bare. But there were new memories made, so, in a way, the world was different. People sighed in relief as the last snow melted while the children looked at the window, forlorn. It was a new world, even though it did not look like it. So, in a way, even though I felt more like myself each day, I felt like a lesser version of who I was. I have always wanted the good and bad in myself, so changing for the better never really seemed enough for me. It was about picking a part of yourself from the women in the cinema but leaving a part of yourself as well. What I have always wanted is this silent communication. Knowing that another person could pick up your qualities like a t-shirt from the lost and found and knowing that it was fine, having this bad side of yourself, leaving it behind, but also realising that you could pick a new bad side the next day.

I never started diaries because I was too scared to finish them. I never knew how to end things so I was always on the edge about starting them. The thing is I am not scared of things ending; I know for a fact that sometimes it is good to run. But, I cannot ignore that I had to tell them to leave me alone and they never did, so it must have been my fault, right? I didn't know how to end things. And when I finally left, I didn't leave with grace. It wasn't an outburst, no. I left without saying anything, without hoping, without loving. It was silence and it spoke volumes even though there was a point in my life when I didn't believe it.

I don't know if I'm someone I hate or if I'm just growing. Someone new or someone I don't know; I'm just fed up of chasing something and realising I will never get it. Giving up always felt like a curse; it was a whisper in my ear. Sometimes I listened. Sometimes I didn't. I didn't have a reason for this; maybe I never will. I just wanted to be good. I wish I could talk more about it but words just seem counterproductive. I'll just keep them inside me because diaries always destroyed me.

Listen to the End (The Vulture Circle)

In my world, girls get replaced every day. My mother sang a haunting lullaby in the final month before I was born; it sounded too much like reality. In the lullaby, a girl stood over bare ground; the dry weather was like a warning sign that all wasn't well. But the girl didn't move and the vultures had caught her stare. In the lullaby, the girl fell into eternal sleep as the sun set. My mother's voice echoed in the bare nursery that my parents were supposed to decorate that day but my father died. I never knew that the lullaby existed until my childhood curiosity led me to my mother's closet with boxes full of the world's best jewels: photos and papers. The lullaby was written in hasty handwriting as if whoever wrote it was too scared that the lullaby would erase from their memory. And I never knew what eternal sleep meant until I was ten, in my mother's car, finally realising. In my world, girls get replaced every day and there are no other rules.

Back when I was twelve years old, I had my first taste of what my mother and I referred to as the Vulture Circle. A girl is born with a vulture circling overhead which increases over the years. In the hospital, why does the mother cry out at the same time the girl does? Why does the mother look at the girl with regret rather than happiness? Because all hospitals reek of possibility but also of inevitability. Because the mother thought the daughter would be safe, but the vultures circle overhead. All girls are born under the Vulture Circle. But when I was twelve, the vultures drew blood from my forehead. They reminded me time and time again that just as the Vulture Circle lore will never leave me, neither will the idea that I have to be a mother.

Girls: what haunting lullabies. Letters found in the shoe box in your mother's closet. Lores in the passenger seat of the car. All things said in passing. Flammable. Expendable. Girls: what short obituaries in the newspaper written out of obligation. Know that when you reach the top, it will only be for a short time. Know that when they tell you, you can be everything, they mean everything but forceful, loud and broken. They mean everything but the girl who gets to stay. You cannot outrun the vultures; new things look so much prettier than old ones and for a moment, you think you will outlive all the vultures above your head. But listen. Girls: what dead things. You don't know you're gone until the newspapers start talking about you as the person you used to be. A vulture never tells you when to run and so I never knew when it would be the time to go.

I have had a recurring dream lately; I am about to turn twenty. The world is huge, but I am standing near the edge of a cliff. Overhead, the vultures circle. I'm scared to look up because I know all that I will see are people who made it faster than me. People who will stay up there for a long, long time. The vultures fill this echoing place in a way that I can hear it even in my heartbeat. Each shadow on the beige soil takes me back to the time in high school when I knew the end was near. Time stays for no one, but especially not for girls. The vultures swoop down, their shadows overpower mine. I wake up at that moment, knowing how it will end. The lullaby still haunts me. And I know a vulture only knows how to draw blood. How to swoop in—at a time that will always feel wrong—and leave all the remains on the floor. It only knows how to steal. And a vulture can steal your youth even when you're young. There is nothing more sure in this world other than the fact that no girl sticks around for long. I never knew twenty could be so old.

I have always known that in a sense, I am quite expendable. As if youth is a currency but I never knew it until they told me it was. And I'll be there at all the dinner parties and the competitions each year, on that stage, knowing I did something but I could be better. Just for them to tell me my time is up even when I'm not done. Just for another girl to come and become the next big thing until the only thing each girl knows is the bottom. I sang the lullaby as I drove back home, the dinner party dress wrapping around my legs. I wish my mother could have seen me in that dress, could have known that the lullaby walked with me to the stage when she should have.

My house was a lone cottage in the middle of nowhere; I inherited it from my mother. I hadn't entered the nursery for a long time.

The room was still bare but this time the lullaby was framed on the wall as if my mother knew I would come back no matter what. As if she knew I needed to see it again. The Vulture Circle stemmed from a mother and her lullaby and then conversations in the car. It was a lullaby but nothing more. But then why does it feel so real? Why did I know so much when I was in high school, the day I had sworn with my best friends that we would never fade away because someone told us to? Each night, the promise shatters. And why do I know nothing now, when all the control I had has gone away?

The cliffs were close to home and I needed to get away. I wish I could say that it didn't remind me of the lullaby and that it didn't draw me in. But I have been feeling desperation for a long time and wanted to feel something else again. The rush on the cliffs, the wind in my hair. It was beautiful; it felt like my time would never end. I took the lullaby with me; I wanted to burn away its mark on me. This naivety had never come back after that trip to California with my mother. And I had loved California on that road trip back when I was sixteen. I can't go back there anymore. The bridges looked too tall; the world seemed mine to keep. My mother had reminded me of the Vulture Circle then, the day she lay dying on the streets as the result of the gun of a man. She sang the lullaby again; this time it was me holding her body. Naivety bore its heart to me but my mother slashed it away. Remember, the vultures only multiply as you grow older. Remember, the only time the vultures will like you is if you're gone. California was beautiful, but I can never go back.

I walked to the cliffs that day. The weather had been perfect for clearing my head. I couldn't help but reminisce as the time passed. The sun was bright, and I didn't look up. But the shadows multiplied; I wish it would have all been in my head. The sun drew tears from my eyes. I wish I hadn't screamed; I wish I wouldn't have remained stuck. The Vulture Circle was right there ever since I was born; I hadn't realised that somehow it had come closer. At the wrong time, at the wrong place. Why reach the top if it all fades away? I never had an answer to this question; I still don't. In my world, the lullabies continue to haunt you even when you stop hearing them, and letters can burn easily. I have known all along but I wish I didn't, so that somehow I would be less disappointed in myself. Disappointed by the fact I hadn't reached the top, disappointed by the fact I never stood in defiance. I was snatched away from my mother's body when the police came but I wish I hadn't listened. But this hurt has been living in my body ever since I was born. I know, in my world, girls get replaced every day.

I hope you have it in you to miss me too.

www.ingramcontent.com/pod-product-compliance
Lightning Source LLC
La Vergne TN
LVHW041127150826
845673LV00007B/2207